D0487872

For Melly – M.M.

First published in 2003 by Macmillan Children's Books
a division of Macmillan Publishers Limited
20 New Wharf Road, London N1 9RR
Basingstoke and Oxford
Associated companies worldwide
www.panmacmillan.com

ISBN 0 333 96230 3 (HB)
ISBN 0 333 96502 7 (PB)

Text copyright © 2003 Miriam Moss
Illustrations copyright © 2003 Jutta Bücker
Moral rights asserted

All rights reserved. No part of this publication may be reproduced, stored in or
introduced into a retrieval system, or transmitted, in any form, or by any means
(electronic, mechanical, photocopying, recording or otherwise) without the prior written
permission of the publisher. Any person who does any unauthorised act in relation to this
publication may be liable to criminal prosecution and civil claims for damages.

1 3 5 7 9 8 6 4 2

A CIP catalogue record for this book is available from the British Library.

Printed in Belgium by Proost

Miriam Moss

The Best Dog in the World

Illustrated by Jutta Bücker

MACMILLAN CHILDREN'S BOOKS

In a small street on a high hill stand two houses, side by side.

Henry lives with his mum and dad in one house. Harvey lives with Grandad in the other.

Harvey is a big dog who pretends to be brave. He barks loudly and guards the gate.

But really he's scared of the postman, thunderstorms and even cats!

Most of all, Harvey is scared of children. When Henry visits Grandad, Harvey shuts himself in the bedroom.

Henry is a little boy who also pretends to be brave. He climbs trees, walks along walls and swings higher than anyone else.

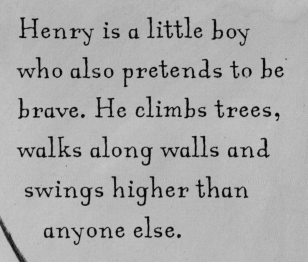

But really he's scared of monsters, getting lost and the dark.

Most of all, Henry is scared of dogs. When Grandad visits Henry, Harvey stays at home.

One day, on Grandad's birthday,
Mum made a picnic and they
all got into the car.

Henry looked out of one window.
Harvey looked out of the other.

At the top of the hill, Grandad parked the car.
"Here we are!" he said.
Henry and Harvey jumped out, raced round
the car — and bumped right into each other.
They took one look and shot off
in opposite directions.

Mum and Dad laid out the picnic
while Henry and Harvey explored.

"Come and get it!" shouted Dad, just as
a gust of wind blew the napkins away.

"Hen-reeey!" called Mum, as the sky grew dark.
"Haaar-vey!" called Grandad, as the first spots of
rain plopped on to the tablecloth.
But the wind snatched their voices away.
And then it poured.

Henry was down at the bottom of the hill
watching puddles grow.

CRACK!

A flash of lightning lit the sky.

Henry raced to a
small barn nearby.

The door creaked
shut behind him.

Henry stood in the dark, his heart thumping.
He reached out and felt his way along a wall.

Something moved. Henry froze.
A dark head and two eyes appeared.

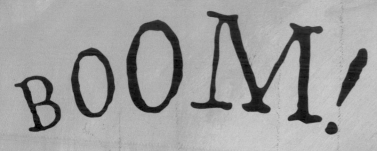

BOOM!

Thunder crashed overhead. Henry jumped.
The thing near him whimpered, and the whole barn
was lit by a great flash of lightning.
Harvey stared at Henry. Henry stared at Harvey.

Harvey was trembling, so Henry spoke
into the dark. "I'm scared, too."
And slowly he stretched out his hand
towards the dog.

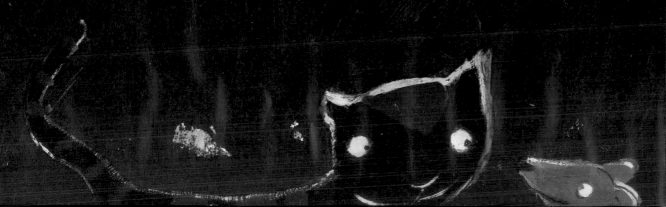

At first Harvey shrank away, but then
he crept back and licked the hand gently.
Very slowly, Harvey moved closer, and
then closer, to Henry.

All around the storm raged,
while Henry stroked Harvey.
Soon Harvey's head was resting
in Henry's lap. Henry sighed,
breathing in the warm dog smell.

And when the storm was over,
that's how Grandad found them,
all curled up and fast asleep in the straw.

Now, when Henry visits Harvey,
Harvey bowls him over.

And when Harvey visits Henry, Henry lifts
his feathery ear and reminds him that he's
the best dog in the whole, wide world.